The Mystery of Miss King

The
Mystery of Miss King

Margaret Ryan
Illustrated by Kate Pankhurst

A & C Black • London

For Isabel and Granny Elspeth with love

First published 2009 by
A & C Black Publishers Ltd
36 Soho Square, London, W1D 3QY

www.acblack.com

Text copyright © 2009 Margaret Ryan
Illustrations copyright © 2009 Kate Pankhurst

ISBN 978-1-4081-0492-7

A CIP catalogue for this book is available from the British Library.

Printed and bound in Great Britain
by CPI Cox & Wyman, Reading, RG1 8EX.

The problem: My old bike. I am growing too big for it, but we can't afford a new one as Dad is off work with a broken leg.

The brainwave: Ask Mr Maini at the corner shop if he has a paper round so I can save up for some new wheels.

The dilemma: There is a paper round, but it takes in Weir Street and I've heard that the people who live there are weird.

The hero: Me, of course. Jonny Smith. I'm not scared – it's only a paper round. And just how weird can the people in Weir Street be...?

Chapter One

I was having breakfast and just about to set off on my paper round, when Mum came into the kitchen carrying a pile of dirty washing.

"Your bedroom is such a mess, Jonny Smith," she said. "I could hardly walk across the floor. You must tidy it up when you come home from school."

"OK," I sighed. It would take a while. I'm just not a very tidy person.

Unlike Miss Violet King, who lives at number 57 Weird Street. Her house always looks spick and span, and her garden is perfect. All the flowers stand to attention, the bushes grow neatly, and the trees never seem to drop their leaves. Her front gate is polished and the path freshly swept. I try not to get any mud on it as I walk along, and when I reach the front door, I open the shiny letter box wearing gloves. For two reasons:

1. So I don't leave any fingerprints.

2. So it doesn't nip my fingers when it springs back.

I don't often see Miss King, which is just as well. She kept me late for school last week. She had written out a list of magazines she wanted to order from Mr Maini, then couldn't find it.

8

"That's strange," she frowned. "I'm sure I put it on the hall table. I'll just go and look for it."

She was away for ages while I hopped about from foot to foot looking at my watch. My teacher, Miss Dodds, goes bananas when I'm late. Which is quite often.

When Miss King finally *did* find the list, there was only half of it left. The rest of it was in her dog, so she had to write it out all over again. In very neat writing.

Then she'd looked at me and said, "Why don't you pull up your socks and tuck in your shirt? A tidy outside means a tidy inside, you know." And she'd tapped her head.

I thought she was crazy. But, crazy or not, I still had to deliver her paper.

❧

I finished my breakfast, said goodbye to Mum and jumped onto my bike. I collected my big orange bag from Mr Maini at the corner shop and set off on my round.

It was a bright morning and, even on my old bike, I enjoyed whizzing down Barr Avenue. But it wasn't such fun pedalling up the big hill to Weird Street.

Captain Cross-eyed at number 13 gave me a wave as he went off to work in the park. "How's the bike fund coming along?" he called.

"Nearly there," I gasped. I couldn't wait to get my new bike. The one I wanted had lots of gears and would make going up Weird Street much easier.

Mr Tipp was in the garden of number 34 and a half when I arrived. I handed him his paper and stopped for a chat.

"What are you inventing now, Mr Tipp?" I asked.

"Something I think could be great fun, Jonny," he grinned. "Bouncing wellies."

"Bouncing wellies?"

"Like these ones I'm wearing," he said. "Watch."

He flicked a remote control and began bouncing around the garden. Then he gave an extra large bounce, leapt over the garden gate and headed down the hill.

"They're not quite right yet," he called. "Now, where's the OFF button?"

I smiled as he disappeared. Mr Tipp always cheered me up.

When I reached Miss King's house, I parked my bike very carefully, so it didn't lean on the hedge, and pushed open the silent gate. The bad-tempered letter box gleamed on the front door, as did the Viking-ship brass knocker.

I put on my gloves and searched in my bag for Miss King's paper. I soon found it, but there was also a whole bundle of magazines with number 57 written on the top right-hand corner. I'd have to put them through the letter box one by one!

It took ages as my gloved fingers kept slipping on the shiny covers. But the magazines all went through, until the last one. It was called *Human Anatomy* and was really thick. I had to give it a huge push.

Big mistake. The front cover ripped in two.

"Oh no," I groaned. Now I would have to knock on the door and apologise. Otherwise Miss King might complain to Mr Maini. I didn't want to lose my job. Not now I was so close to being able to afford a new bike.

I lifted the heavy knocker and gave a tap. Nothing happened. I banged a little harder. Still no one answered.

I must have leaned on the door when I knocked, because it slid open silently, and I found myself looking into an empty hall. The scattered magazines and paper lay on the floor beside the morning post. A large pot plant sat neatly on the hall table, but I couldn't see or hear anything. Not the radio or the TV, not Miss King, or even her dog. There seemed to be no one around except me.

"Hello," I called. "Hello? Is anybody there?"

Nothing.

I chewed on my lip. Something was wrong. Miss King would never leave her house unattended. Never leave her front door open for anyone to walk in. It was all very strange and I wondered what I should do.

Chapter Two

I decided to have a look round the back.
Miss King was probably outside washing
her wheelie bin, or ironing the grass.

I tiptoed round the side of the house,
past the the stone Viking warrior peeping
out from behind the water butt, and past
the two Viking gods fiercely guarding the
compost heap. Which was tidy, of course.

There was no Miss King. But there *was*
a shed. Checking that no one was looking,
I sprinted across the grass and peered in
the window.

Inside, I could see a white-painted chair,
a grey filing cabinet and a large wooden
workbench. On the bench, laid out in rows,

were some strange tools, and beside them lay some old sacks, which were neatly folded. Then I saw another sack sitting on the floor. It was lumpy and bulging, and there was something sticking out of it. I gasped, rubbed my eyes, and craned my neck to have a closer look. What was sticking out of it was ... a foot!

What? Whose foot was *that*? I didn't wait to find out. I turned and ran. I leapt over the garden gate and jumped on my bike. I quickly delivered my other papers, and was still breathing hard when I handed in my bag to Mr Maini.

"Are you all right, Jonny?" he asked. "You look like you've seen a ghost."

"No, not a ghost," I said, and decided to say no more. Mr Maini hadn't believed me when I'd told him about the enormous pirate who lived at number 13, and this story was even more unlikely.

So I just got back on my bike and headed for school.

I got there in record time.

Miss Dodds was surprised to see me. "You're early this morning, Jonny," she said. "Threatening to ban you from football practice seems to have worked. You may get to play in the inter-schools' football final on Saturday, after all."

I gave her a weak smile and slumped down in my seat. I wasn't going to tell her what I'd just seen; she *never* believed me.

"What's wrong with you?" my friend Surinder grinned, sitting down behind me. "You're not late."

"But you look terrible," said my other friend, Sara. "You haven't seen some Martians land their spacecraft in Weird Street, have you?"

"No," I said. "Trouble is, I'm not sure *what* I've seen. Can't speak now. I'll tell you all about it at break..."

∽∾∿

"Surely it can't have been a *real* foot," said Sara, as we munched our apples in the playground. "Otherwise there would have been a lot of blood. What did it look like?"

"I don't know. A foot," I said, crossly. "A foot attached to a bit of leg."

"Ah," said Surinder. "You didn't say anything before about a leg."

"I've only just remembered."

"What kind of a leg?" asked Sara. "Male or female?"

"I don't know. I was too shocked to notice."

"Was it smooth or hairy?" asked Surinder. "My dad's got really hairy legs."

"Smooth, I think, and brown…"

"See," said Sara. "You *are* remembering. I could be a policeman like your dad. I bet he's good at getting people to remember things."

"Why don't you tell your dad about it and see what he thinks," said Surinder.

"I'm going to, just as soon as I get home," I nodded. But I couldn't get that foot out of my mind. I kept seeing it, sticking up out of the sack, and it put me off my schoolwork.

"You've been staring into space all morning, Jonny Smith," frowned Miss Dodds, when she saw how few maths problems I had done. "You'll finish these at home."

"OK," I sighed, and put my maths book into my rucksack. I'd have to do them after I tidied my room.

Mr McGregor, our football coach, wasn't too pleased with me at practice, either.

"You're on another planet, today, Smith," he yelled. "Keep your eye on the ball if you want to keep your place in the team."

"Uh huh," I muttered, and did my best, but I couldn't wait to get home to tell Dad what I'd seen.

In the end, I told Mum and Gran, too, as they were all sitting in the kitchen.

"Are you sure about this, Jonny?" frowned Dad, when I'd finished. "You've told us some strange stories about the people in Weir Street before."

"But they all turned out to be true," Mum pointed out.

"The enormous pirate, the wacky inventor, the mysterious archaeologist…" Gran ticked them off on her fingers. "And now… Did you know that in the nineteenth century there were two men called Burke and Hare, who were grave robbers. They used to dig up the bodies then sell the parts to medical science."

"That's quite enough of that." Dad was stern. "I'm sure there's a perfectly simple explanation. The foot's probably a theatrical prop, or something from a joke shop."

"But you could check the missing persons register," Gran said. "Just to be sure."

"You watch too many cop shows," sighed Dad. "But I'll drop by the station tomorrow, if you like."

"Excellent," said Gran. "I love a good mystery."

She wasn't the only one. Sara phoned me later that evening.

"Surinder and I have been talking," she said. "We've decided you shouldn't go back to Miss King's on your own, so we'll help with your paper round tomorrow."

"But you two hate getting up early," I said. "I bet you just want to have a look in that shed."

"Maybe," said Sara. "But I don't hear you complaining."

She was right. I would be glad of their company. Just in case...

Chapter Three

"What do you know about Miss King at number 57?" I asked Mr Maini, while I was waiting for Sara and Surinder to arrive.

"Not a lot." Mr Maini shook his head. "She hasn't lived in the street very long, but she seems nice enough. She has a big, shaggy dog called Thor. He comes in here with her to buy dog food. And she orders loads of magazines. Which reminds me, I have another one for her today." He took it from under the counter and popped it in my orange bag. But not before I'd seen the title: *Ancient Burial Grounds*.

I swallowed hard. What did she want to know about *them* for? Fortunately, at that moment Sara and Surinder arrived, so I went outside to meet them.

"Let's go to number 57 first," said Sara. "I can't wait to sneak a look at that foot."

"OK," I agreed. "I'll be glad to get it over with."

We pedalled right up to the top of the hill to Miss King's house.

"You didn't tell us the garden was full of Vikings!" exclaimed Surinder.

"Did you know that, starting around the eighth century, the Vikings terrorised Europe for about 200 years?" said Sara.

I tried to ignore her. Sara can be a bit of a brainbox sometimes and likes to show off what she knows, but I'd been terrified enough by the sight of that foot! "I'll go and knock on the front door," I said. "If Miss King's in, I'll apologise for ripping the magazine yesterday. If not, I'll wave and we can slip round to the shed and have a look."

"Good plan," breathed Sara.

Sara and Surinder waited while I hurried up the path. I took a deep breath and rapped on the door.

No reply.

I tried again.

Still no reply.

I pushed the paper through the letter box and leaned on the door. It didn't open. I leaned a bit harder. It still didn't move.

"Looks like she's out," I said, and gave my friends a wave.

Sara and Surinder came running.

We sneaked round the path, past the Viking warrior and the Viking gods. They eyed us sternly.

"Don't tell anyone we were here," I said.

"You're getting to be as weird as the people who live in this street," muttered Surinder.

Single file, we crept up to the shed and peeked in.

The white-painted chair was there. The grey filing cabinet was there. The wooden table with the strange tools was there. But there was no foot sticking out of a lumpy, bulging sack. All the sacks were neatly folded ... and empty.

Sara and Surinder sighed deeply. "Are you sure you saw a foot?" said Sara. "Maybe it was your imagination. You *can* be a bit dozy sometimes."

"Or maybe it was a trick of the light," said Surinder, when he saw me scowl. "Anyway, there's nothing there now, so there's no point in us sticking around."

Then they both shrugged and headed for their bikes.

"OK," I muttered. I didn't know whether to be disappointed or relieved. I was about to set off to deliver the rest of my papers, when I remembered the *Ancient Burial Grounds* magazine. It was still in my bag.

I went round to the front of the house and was just about to push it through the letter box when a voice behind me said.

"I'll take that. I don't want it torn, like yesterday's."

It was Miss King!

She stood there, very tall and straight, with her fair hair scraped back in a long plait. In one hand she held a bag and, in the other, the lead of a large dog.

"I'm s-s-s-sorry about the magazine," I stuttered. "I thought it would go through the letter box, but it didn't."

"Just knock next time," she said, putting down her bag while she fished in her pocket for her keys.

The dog slumped onto the ground and nosed open the bag.

"Leave, Thor!" commanded Miss King.

Thor took no notice. Instead, he pawed at the contents, scraping back a piece of white paper. Miss King pulled him away quickly, but not before I'd glimpsed what was underneath. To my horror, it was a large *bone* and it still had some flesh clinging to it. Could it possibly be human, I wondered?

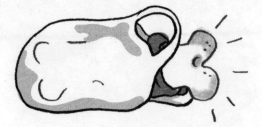

Chapter Four

I did the rest of my paper round with my mind in a whirl. First I'd seen a foot, now a bone. What *was* Miss King up to?

I couldn't stop thinking about it all the way to school, and I wondered if I should tell Sara and Surinder. They hadn't really been convinced I'd seen a foot...

I decided to take the chance.

"A *bone*?" said Sara at break. "What kind of bone?"

"I don't know," I muttered. "It was long."

"Like an arm bone or a leg bone?" asked Surinder.

"I don't know," I repeated. "It didn't exactly have a label on it."

"Could it have belonged to the foot you *say* you saw the other day?" asked Sara. "Or is this just another one of your stories?"

"I *did* see a foot *and* a bone. You're as bad as Miss Dodds!"

I was cross. Cross because I knew what I'd seen, but no one seemed to believe me. Not even my friends. What was I to do? I thought about it for a while, then decided to put all ideas of feet and bones out of my mind for good.

But Gran wouldn't let me.

When I got home from school, she was there again. She handed me a library book.

"It's about Burke and Hare. I thought you might be interested. In case you've seen any more body parts…"

"Well…" I said, and then I told her about the bone.

Dad, who was reading his newspaper, got cross. "Stop this nonsense, both of you," he said. "I checked with the station and there are no missing persons around here. Now, why don't you be sensible, Jonny, and concentrate on winning this football match on Saturday instead."

"OK," I said. I'd be happy to.

But it wasn't that easy. Next morning, Mr Maini had another thick magazine for Miss King.

"She certainly has some unusual interests," he said, handing it to me.

I looked at the title and gulped. *The Muscles of the Human Body*. I daren't think what she wanted *that* for!

I stuck it in my bag, along with the rest of the papers, and set off on my round. Outside number 36, I met Dr Sphinx. He was putting a large bag into the back of a taxi.

"Hello, Jonny," he smiled. "I'm glad I met you. Will you ask Mr Maini to cancel my paper till I get back from Egypt. I forgot."

"Of course," I nodded. "Have a good trip."

"I'll send you a postcard," he said, and got into the taxi. It was only when it had disappeared down the hill that I wished I'd asked Dr Sphinx if he knew anything about Miss King.

I carried on with my round, but when I got to number 57 and tried to put the magazine through the snappy letter box, it wouldn't fit.

"Oh no," I said. "Not again!" There was nothing for it. I'd have to knock on the door.

I banged the knocker.

No reply.

I thought about taking the magazine back to the shop, but then I'd *still* have to deliver it tomorrow.

Then I had another thought. Perhaps I could leave it on the window ledge, weighed down by the Viking gods.

I went over to the compost heap. "Excuse me," I said, picking them up, "but I need you to guard something else today."

I put the magazine on the ledge and sat the stone gods on top. "You can look in the window, if you like," I said, and turned them round.

I wish I hadn't, for there, grinning at us from the top of the TV, was a human skull…

"Aaaargh!" I yelled and bolted down the path. It was getting to be quite a habit. I suppose I must have finished the rest of my round, but I don't really remember. I just know that when I got back to Mr Maini's my bag was empty.

"What's wrong, Jonny?" said Mr Maini. "You look upset."

"It's nothing," I said, backing out of the shop. "Just got some things on my mind."

I must be sensible, I must be sensible, I kept repeating. Dad's sure to be right.

There are no missing persons from around here. The skull's probably a theatrical prop or maybe a plastic one from a joke shop. The trouble was, it didn't look plastic. It looked only too real. Those staring eyes. Those tombstone teeth...

"But you can't tell anyone about it," I said out loud, as I pedalled to school. "Or they'll really think you're nuts. Just try to do as Dad says and concentrate on Saturday's game."

Chapter Five

So I did. I tried to put it all out of my mind and for the next couple of days luckily there were no more magazines to deliver. I just stuck Miss King's paper through her letter box and hurried away as fast as I could.

Finally, Saturday arrived and the long-awaited inter-schools' football final. I was really nervous; so were the rest of the team. Only Mr McGregor was calm.

"Just do your best, lads," he told us in the dressing room. "Remember all I've taught you and you'll be fine. And, Smith, you keep your eye on the ball. Don't let your mind wander."

"OK," I said. If only he knew!

We started off well, with Peter Ho scoring the first goal. Our supporters, which included Captain Cross-eyed and Mr Tipp, cheered, but then the other team scored, and their supporters cheered. That happened again and it was 2–2. I knew Mum and Dad and Ellie, my little sister, were on the touchline, but I was determined to stay focussed, and I tried not to look at them.

At last, the referee blew his whistle for half-time and we trooped back to the dressing room.

Mr McGregor spoke. "You're doing fine, lads," he said. "But we need that extra push. Dig deep and give it all you've got."

We nodded and ran back out onto the field, determined to play our socks off. And we did. But the other team were good. Very good. We were getting tired and struggling to hold on.

The referee looked at his watch and I heard Mr McGregor yell, "Come on, lads, just one minute to go!"

Then it happened. I'm not sure how, but suddenly the ball was at my feet and I had a clear sight of the goal. I let fly and really connected with the ball. It soared into the air, over the heads of the other players and hit the side of the post. I held my breath. The ball bounced in.

All our supporters yelled and jumped into the air. Mr Tipp jumped higher than everyone else, so I guess he must have been wearing his bouncing wellies, and Captain Cross-eyed tossed up his pirate hat. My dad couldn't jump with his broken leg, so he waved his crutch instead.

The final whistle blew. All our hours of practice had paid off. We had won the inter-schools' football championship! I could hardly believe it. Neither could Mr McGregor. He couldn't stop grinning. "Well done, lads," he kept saying. "Well done. I knew you could do it."

Mrs Bone from the council presented each of us with a medal, then we did a lap of honour with the cup. It felt great, and somehow we weren't tired any more. After that, Mr McGregor took the whole team out for a pizza to celebrate. I had mine with extra pepperoni and cheese, then washed it down with lots of Coke.

When I got home, Mum gave me a big hug and Dad congratulated me and showed me the pictures he'd taken of the game.

"Great goal, Jonny," he smiled. "You saw your chance and took it. You've got a really useful right foot there. Keep practising with it." And he ruffled my hair.

I could tell he was pleased.

Chapter Six

I got up extra early on Monday morning. Mr McGregor had promised we could take the cup round the school to show it off, and I didn't want to miss any of that.

I delivered my papers as fast as I could. When I got to Miss King's, the house was silent. There was no sign of Miss King or her dog, and I wasn't going anywhere near the shed! But one thing *was* different – there was a large hole in the middle of the front lawn.

"That's odd," I muttered. "Everything's usually so neat and tidy. Perhaps she's rearranging the garden... Or burying something," I added.

But I was supposed to be being sensible, so I pushed that thought away.

The team had a great time going round all the classes, holding the cup above our heads and listening to the cheers. It was ages before we got back to our desks.

"There you are at last," said Miss Dodds. "I'm very pleased you won the inter-schools' football championship, but now the contest is over, maybe we can get some proper work done around here."

We tried, but it wasn't easy. Everyone was too excited. A reporter came round to interview the team and we had our photo in the local paper. Mr McGregor cut it out and pinned it up on the school notice board.

Things were quieter after that. Quite flat, really, with no football practice and nothing else to look forward to. Miss Dodds made us work really hard and we were getting a bit fed up.

"We could do with some of your fantastic stories to cheer us up, Jonny," said Surinder. "What's been happening in Weird Street?"

I took a deep breath. Did I want to bring it up all over again? Should I say something, or not?

"Nothing much has been going on..." I began. "Dr Sphinx has gone to help excavate an Egyptian tomb, Captain Cross-eyed is busy painting the pirate ship in the park, and Mr Tipp is inventing something that produces lots of purple smoke. So I haven't seen much of them." Actually, it would have been good to find out what they knew about the mysterious Miss King.

"So it's all quite normal then," Surinder sounded disappointed.

"Yes, unless..."

"Unless *what*?" Sara's eyes gleamed.

"Unless you count the *skull* I saw in Miss King's sitting room and the large holes that have started appearing in her front garden. First there was only one, but now they're all over the place."

"Skull?" said Sara. "Why didn't you tell us before?"

I shrugged. "I was fed up of no one believing me."

"Maybe the holes are for new flower beds," said Surinder.

"Maybe," I said.

"Some workmen may be putting in a pipe, or something," said Sara.

"Possibly. It's just…"

"What?"

"It's such a mess. Miss King is so neat and tidy. I don't think anyone would dare leave her garden in that state."

"Maybe something is going on," said Sara, thoughtfully. "Maybe you *did* see a mysterious foot and a strange bone and a skull, after all…"

"Maybe it needs to be investigated," said Surinder. "Maybe the holes are to bury some body parts…"

"Oh no," I said. "I'm not starting that again. I got a telling-off from my dad the last time I mentioned it. And I haven't seen any more bits of body."

"Probably because you haven't looked," said Sara.

"Too scared, I bet," said Surinder.

That made me cross, so the next morning when I got to number 57, I took a deep breath and had a quick look in the holes.

They were all empty.

I breathed a sigh of relief and started to push the paper into Miss King's letter box. But some post was stuck in there already. I bent down to poke through a large envelope and saw into the hall. It was empty, but something strange caught my eye. I gasped. My throat went dry and my knees turned to jelly. I didn't see any body parts, but hanging on the end of the banister was something long, grey and straggly. It looked to me very much like human hair...

Chapter Seven

I got such a fright, I wobbled and fell backwards onto the path. I was just getting up when the door opened. Miss King was standing there with Thor.

"What about my paper?" she asked.

Oh no, I was still holding it! I scrambled to my feet and, with a shaking hand, held out the paper.

"Can you come a bit nearer," said Miss King. "I don't bite."

I inched closer, then I noticed she was leaning heavily on crutches. "You've got the same plaster as my dad!" I exclaimed.

She looked down and sighed. "I was tackled too hard playing American football. Fell and broke my leg."

"American football?"

Miss King nodded and gestured to the hall table. I didn't go any closer, but I could see that beside the pot plant sat a football helmet with the word "Vikings" written on it. "That's my team. But I love anything to do with Vikings. Probably because of my name, Vi King," she laughed. "But the team will have to do without me for a while. So will the museum, though at least I can continue with some work at home."

"You work at the museum?" I asked, my curiosity getting the better of me.

"Yes. There's to be a Viking exhibition soon and I'm making the life-sized models for it. There are bits of them all over the house and the shed at the moment. That's Freya's hair on the end of the banister. It will go on a real Viking skull as soon as the clay I've used to model the features dries out. I've already finished her body."

"Oh," I said, trying to take everything in. "I saw a bone in your bag the other day."

Miss King laughed again. "That was for Thor. I collected it from the butcher's on our early-morning walk. Trouble is, Thor's not getting his regular walks now, and he's really bored. He's learned how to open the front door and, a week ago, he nosed open the latch and took off.

"I finally caught up with him in Dr Sphinx's garden. Thor likes Dr Sphinx's cats, but they're not so keen on him! And now he's making a real mess digging around in my garden. Unfortunately, there's nothing I can do about it till my leg mends."

Suddenly everything became clear. The foot, the bone, the skull and the holes in the garden. Even the kind of magazines Miss King had ordered.

I felt a bit silly about my suspicions and was really glad she didn't know what

I'd been thinking. Then I had one of my brilliant ideas. That happens to me sometimes. I think I may be an undiscovered genius.

"I play football, too," I said.

"I know," smiled Miss King. "I saw your photo in the paper. Your team won the inter-schools' championship. Well done."

"Thank you. But now, after all the excitement, things are a bit dull. We've never played American football at school. Do you think, if I walked your dog for you, you could come and teach us?"

"Hmm," Miss King was thoughtful. "That's a good idea, and I certainly know where we could borrow the necessary equipment. I'd like that, and Thor would love the walks."

"I'll have to speak to Mr McGregor, our coach, but I'm sure he'll agree. He loves any kind of sport."

At school, I went to see Mr McGregor right away. As I thought, he was really keen.

"Great idea," he said. "Ask Miss King to call me and I'll see what we can arrange. Perhaps we could start lunchtime practices again." Then he went off, whistling.

I went off to my classroom, late again.

Miss Dodds' eyes narrowed when I arrived. "Well," she said. "What kept you today? And I don't want one of your usual silly stories."

"OK," I said, and missed out the 'I thought Miss King might be a body snatcher' bit, and went straight to the 'I went to see Mr McGregor to tell him one of the people on my paper round was interested in teaching us American football' bit.

Then I waited for the explosion. *Too much football and not enough work! How do you expect to pass exams?* Etc, etc.

But the explosion didn't come. Instead, Miss Dodds actually smiled. "American football? Now there's an exciting game. I wouldn't mind having a go at it myself. Well done, Jonny. That's a great idea."

What?

The class were stunned into complete silence. And I still haven't got over it.

Mr McGregor arranged to collect Miss King at lunchtimes and our coaching started right away.

In exchange, I took Thor out for long walks along with our dog, Brutus. They were great company for each other, and Thor stopped digging holes in Miss King's garden.

Miss King was really pleased and insisted on giving me some money to add to my bike fund.

"You deserve it, Jonny," she smiled.

I thanked her and, when I got home, I took out the rest of my savings and counted them up.

Yippee! I'd finally done it! I'd saved enough money for my new bike.

I went into town at the weekend to buy it. It's bright blue and goes like the wind. I know because I rode it all the way home.

"Will you give up your paper round now you've got your new bike?" asked Dad, when he'd finished admiring it. "After all, that's what you wanted the money for."

"I've thought about that, " I said. "I don't really like getting up early, but I've made some good friends on my round. So I think I'll carry on for a while. Anyway, I'm really curious about the new person who's moved into number 14. Yesterday, I noticed she had a bright-pink broomstick parked outside her front door..."